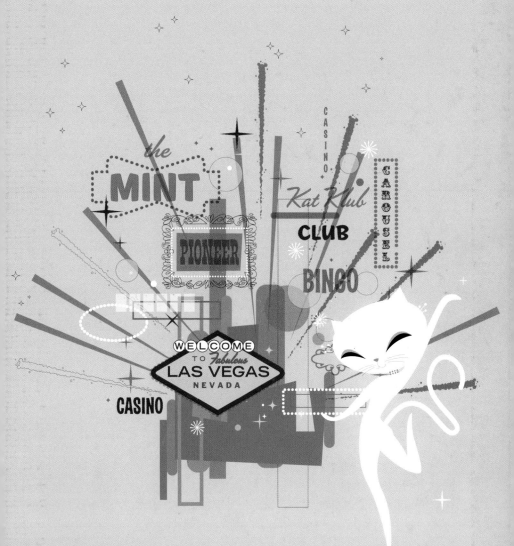

Las Vegas Pair-a-dice

Featuring French Kitty® by Mighty Fine™

Harry N. Abrams, Inc., Publishers

for Marlon

As the big sun dipped
slowly into the west,
Kitty sighed, "Birdie,
I'm getting depressed!

We're so far from New York . . .
we've been driving for days
through landscapes quite strange
with no shops or cafés."

With nighttime descending,
they worried and fretted.
They hadn't a clue where
they were *or* were headed.

As they wondered what else
could go wrong on this day,
their lucky pink dice
blew off and away!

Kitty pulled over.

We've traveled so far and now, more bad luck—there's no gas in the car.

Then off in the distance,
deep into the night,
they spotted the glow
of an orb burning bright.

The light seemed to beckon:
Come closer, come see,
a dreamlike oasis
of fun, fancy-free!

the

MINT

CASINO

Kat Klub

CLUB

CAROUSEL

PIONEER

BINGO

24 HOUR

WELCOME
TO *Fabulous*
LAS VEGAS
NEVADA

CASINO

Viva Las Vegas!
Glitz, glamour, and dames!
Kitty's heart skipped a beat
as she dreamed of the games!

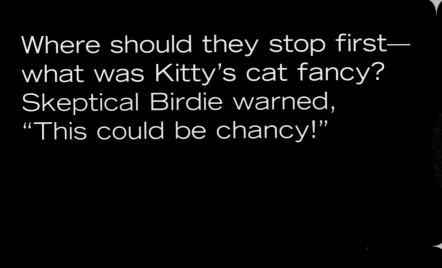

Where should they stop first—
what was Kitty's cat fancy?
Skeptical Birdie warned,
"This could be chancy!"

Come on! Don't be silly!
One bet couldn't hurt.
At least we're escaping
that ol' desert dirt!

the Sandbox

VEGAS
SENSATION
MIDNIGHT
& THE MAGICIAN

OPEN

CASINO HOTEL

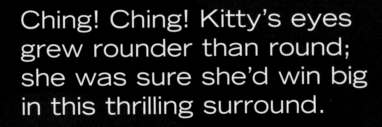

Ching! Ching! Kitty's eyes
grew rounder than round;
she was sure she'd win big
in this thrilling surround.

Kitty, be careful . . .
we've had such bad luck!

She tried slot machines, blackjack, and poker, and such . . . She lost games. She won games. (She didn't win much.)

So taken with gambling,
our misguided honey
kept spending and spending
and spending her money.

From blackjack to poker
to table roulette,
where a smartly clad dealer
said, "Miss, place your bet!"

But how very sad
for our feline French belle . . .
The high roller beside her
was casting a spell.

This cunning bad cat won
the game and then went
out the door leaving Kitty . . .

Not even one cent!

"This road-trip," chirped Birdie,
"is one big disaster!
You couldn't have emptied
your purse any faster!"

Then poor little Birdie,
filled with confusion,
took in what appeared
to be an illusion.

Outside the casino,
on Sin City's curb,
sat a similiar kitty,
as sad and disturbed!

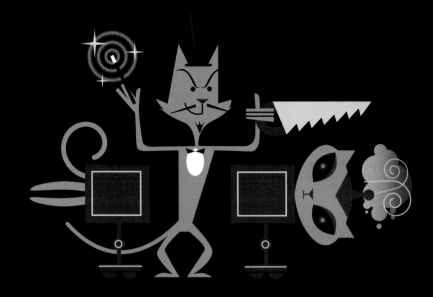

I'm a magician's assistant,
my name is Midnight.
My boss is a crook,
now he's nowhere in sight.

He uses his magic to
dupe and deceive
the innocent, helpless,
and sweetly naïve.

Glitter and glamour!
Pink paint, a big feather!
Don't fret tonight's show—
we'll do it together!

Backstage,
the newly formed feline duet
went over the cues
for their very first set.

The crowd was entranced
by the picturesque vision
of magical moves done with
grace and precision.

Their fantastic feats
surprised even Birdie
and no one had ever
seen costumes so purrrr-dy.

As the two became stars,
overnight, just like that,
who should appear
but the high-rolling cat.

The talented kitties saw
through his sly game—
the high roller and magician
were one and the same!

He slyly observed,
"Your new act's delicious,"
and thought to himself,
Why, this is auspicious.

"With our talents combined,
we'll rake in the money,
a handsome magician
with two lovely honeys!"

"There's only one problem," the kittens revealed,

"This trio's a duo,
our deal is now sealed.

We're called
PINK PAIR-A-DICE!
The strip's newest sensation!
Our act has no need
for a cheating magician."

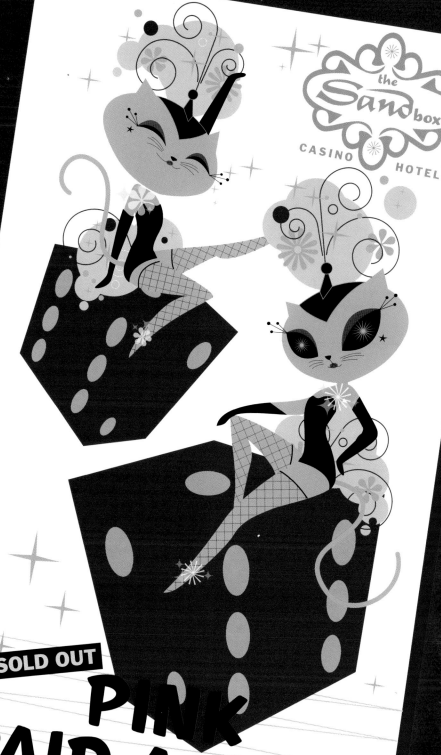

the **Sandbox**

CASINO HOTEL

SOLD OUT

PINK
PAIR-A-DICE

The Strip's Newest Sensation!

The two lucky ladies
concluded their night
with an elegant feast
overlooking the lights.

Then the act hit the road
with Birdie in tow.
New adventures await them,
now on with the show!

Original illustrations and design by Mighty Fine™

Library of Congress Cataloging-in-Publication Data

Mighty Fine.
French Kitty in Las Vegas pair-a-dice / by Mighty Fine.
p. cm.
Summary: After the fashionable feline French Kitty loses all of her
money at a Las Vegas casino, she teams up with another cat to
stage a successful magic show.
ISBN 0-8109-5861-9
1. Cats—Fiction. 2. Las Vegas (Nev.)—Fiction. 3. Stories in rhyme.]
I. Title: Las Vegas pair-a-dice. II. Title.

PZ8.3.M57193 Fr 2005
[Fic]—dc22
2004015608

For more fashion-packed adventures with French Kitty® and her
friends, please visit:

www.french-kitty.com

Published in 2005 by Harry N. Abrams, Incorporated, New York
Printed and bound in China
10 9 8 7 6 5 4 3 2 1

Harry N. Abrams, Inc.
100 Fifth Avenue
New York, NY 10011
www.abramsbooks.com
Abrams is a subsidiary of

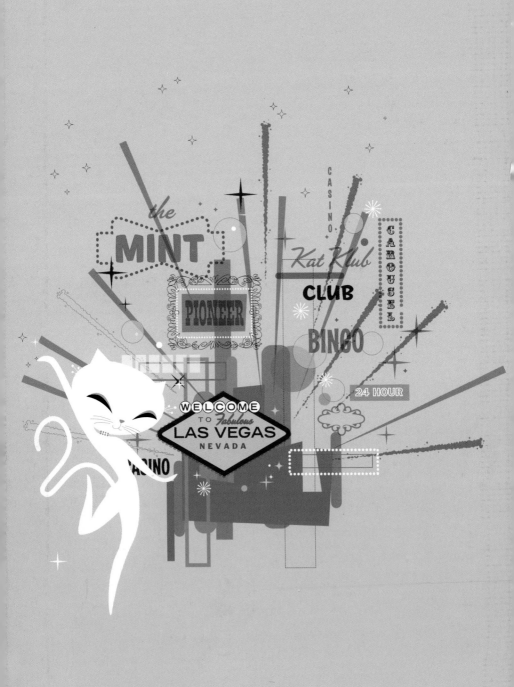